CAPTAIN ABI

TREA

Colin Mc

UL'S LITTLE

SURE

Naughton

WALKER BOOKS
AND SUBSIDIARIES
LONDON · BOSTON · SYDNEY · AUCKLAND

Kaboom!

ONE FINE SUMMER'S MORNING, in a little port on the south coast of England, a pirate ship called *The Golden Behind* was lying at anchor.

The ship belonged to Captain Abdul and his crew. They had come into port to stock up on provisions: rum, gunpowder, sherbet dips – that sort of thing. Later that day, the pirates had an appointment with a Spanish treasure ship. A gentle breeze ruffled the Jolly Roger and fanned the sleeping face of 'Poop-deck' Percy Ploppe – Percy was on watch-duty.

Suddenly, an explosion shattered the peace and a cannonball knocked Percy out of the crow's nest.

"Arrgh!"

roared Captain Abdul, rushing out of his cabin and tripping over a chest. **"Who left that there? An' who be a-disturbin' o' me beauty-sleep firin' cannons? I'll 'ave 'im strung up by 'is ears from the yard-arm, that I will. Ooh-arrgh, by the powers! Oh, me poor leg!"**

The crew came rushing up on deck, which was lucky for Percy,
but not so lucky for the crew.

"**Who be attackin' *The Golden Behind*?**" bellowed the captain.

"**Let me get me 'and on 'im!**" He looked out to sea and saw a ship
disappearing over the horizon. "**Cowards!**" howled Captain Abdul.

"**Come back 'ere an' fight, curse ye! Ooh-arrgh, ye swabs!**"

"Treasure?"

gasped Percy, when he saw the chest. "Maybe it's full of treasure!"

"By the powers!" roared Captain Abdul. **"Why would anyone be leavin' treasure? It's not Christmas!"**

"Maybe we should open it, Cap'n," suggested 'Spanish' Omar Lette.

"Aye!" hissed the captain, a greedy glint in his eye. **"Percy, open it!"**

"But Captain," trembled Percy, "it might not be treasure, it might be something … DANGEROUS!"

"OPEN IT, curse ye!" ordered the captain.

So Percy opened it…

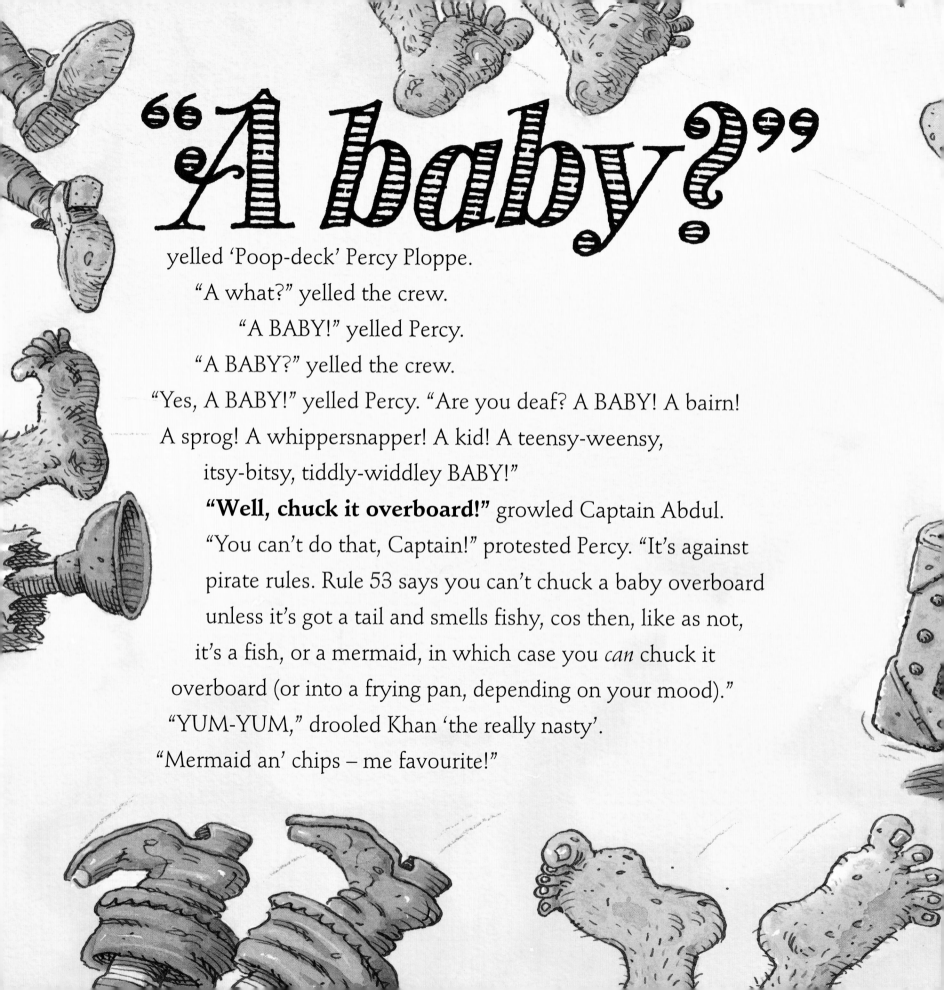

"A baby?"

yelled 'Poop-deck' Percy Ploppe.

"A what?" yelled the crew.

"A BABY!" yelled Percy.

"A BABY?" yelled the crew.

"Yes, A BABY!" yelled Percy. "Are you deaf? A BABY! A bairn! A sprog! A whippersnapper! A kid! A teensy-weensy, itsy-bitsy, tiddly-widdley BABY!"

"Well, chuck it overboard!" growled Captain Abdul.

"You can't do that, Captain!" protested Percy. "It's against pirate rules. Rule 53 says you can't chuck a baby overboard unless it's got a tail and smells fishy, cos then, like as not, it's a fish, or a mermaid, in which case you *can* chuck it overboard (or into a frying pan, depending on your mood)."

"YUM-YUM," drooled Khan 'the really nasty'.

"Mermaid an' chips – me favourite!"

"A note!"

cried Percy. "It was under the baby. It's from your wife, Captain, it's from Mrs Abdul!"

"What!" hissed the captain. **"What does the old battle-axe want?"**

Percy read the note: *"Abdul, I'm fed-up with doing all the work around here while you're out playing with your mates. So, me and the other pirate wives have hired a ship and gone off for a week's pirating. Look after my little treasure while I'm away.*

If one hair on his head is harmed, you hairy great smelly tub of lard, you'll have me to deal with. He takes after me – he's delicate!

Signed, Doris."

"**How could she do this to me?**" howled Captain Abdul. "**I'm a pirate, by the curse o' Blackbeard's flamin' whiskers! How can I make a livin' if I'm stuck 'ere in port lookin' after a baby? What's the woman thinkin' of, dumpin' a ninfant wi' a bunch of fearsome pirates? It's hirrisponsibul, HIRRISPONSIBUL!**"

The baby started crying again.

"Now look what you've done," scolded Percy. "You've upset him with all that shouting. Wassamatter, my lickle baby? Has the big nasty man fwightened you? There, there, my little treasure."

The baby gurgled with pleasure.

"Aahhh," sighed Percy, "isn't he cute?"

"**Course 'e's cute – 'e takes after me!**" said Captain Abdul proudly. "**We're as close as any son an' dad has ever been, ooh-arrgh!**"

"So what's his name?" asked Percy.

"**No idea,**" replied Abdul. "**We're not *that* close!**"

"Avast!"

laughed Captain Abdul. **"Ooh-arrgh, ha-har!"**

"Found him some proper pirate clothes in the stores," declared Percy
proudly. "Must have got shrunked in the wash. Fit 'im perfect!"

The crew cheered.

"What'll we call 'im?" asked Walker 'the plank'. "He needs a pirate nickname."

"How about 'Little Treasure'?" suggested Percy. "After all, we did find
him in a treasure chest."

The crew agreed that this was a fine nickname for a pirate baby.
But the captain started grumbling again: **"I'm Abdul! Captain of *The
Golden Behind*! I'm a pirate! I'm hairy and scary, with more bits
missing than a second-hand jigsaw. I fights. I steals. I drinks rum.
I DO NOT BABY-SIT! I've got my repootashun to think about –
I'll be the laughing-stock of the pirate world."**

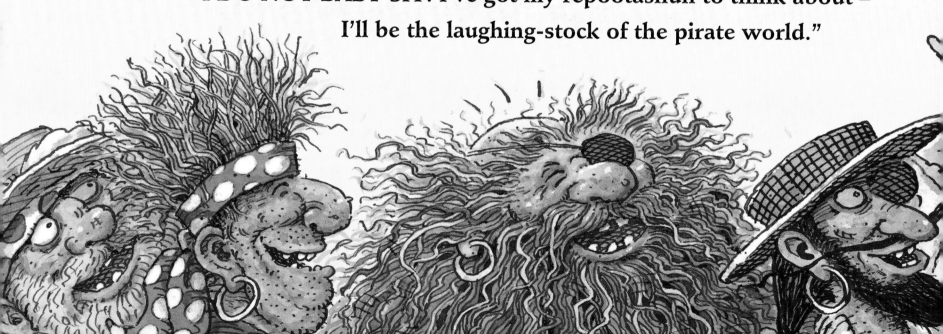

"Oh, come on, Captain,"
said Percy. "It can't be that hard
to look after a baby for a few days."
"Aye, curse it," said Abdul,
**"I suppose yer right. Divide up the
crew into baby-sitting teams, Percy,
make sure 'e's looked after every day."**
"Which day will you be lookin' after 'im,
Captain?" asked Percy innocently.
"ME?" bellowed the captain.
**"Why, ye mutinous dog! I'll
be keepin an eye on y'all.
I'll be sooperavizin!"**
"Hmm," said Percy to himself,
"thought so."

"Pirates!"

bellowed Captain Abdul to his crew.

"Line up and hintroduce yer smelly selves to Little Treasure and tell me what y'know about babies."

When they were finished, the captain, clearly impressed by the depth of their knowledge, declared them all to be **"Baby Hexperts"**.

"Burp!"

burped Little Treasure at dinner that night.

"That'll teach y' t' eat yer sausages so quickly!"
hooted Captain Abdul.

"Swossages!" whooped Little Treasure
and the pirates fell about laughing.

"**Percy,**" slobbered Abdul, "**have y' worked out the baby-sittin' stuff?**"

"Aye, Captain," said Percy. "Me an' the lads have all kinds o' plans."

"**Good!**" growled the captain. "**Cos I'll be sooperavizin! Well, Little Treasure, seven days o' bein' baby-sat by the hairiest, scariest bunch o' pirates this side o' the Spanish main – what d' y' think o' that?**"

"Swossages!" whooped Little Treasure

and the pirates fell about laughing.

"Come 'ere,

y' little villain!" spluttered Captain Abdul.

"Wait till I git me 'and on you!"

Thus were the crew of *The Golden Behind* awakened
the following day at the crack of noon.

"What happened?" gasped 'Portobello' Billy.

**"That little 'ooligan there sawed me
wooden leg off when I were asleep!"**
thundered Abdul.

"Good job 'e didn't go fer
yer good leg, Cap'n,"
grinned Billy and the
pirates fell about laughing.

Today it was Walker 'the
plank' and 'I'm alright'
Jack's turn to
baby-sit, so, as
Abdul hopped off
to get a spare leg,

they showed Little Treasure how to tie sailor-type knots. He turned
out to be rather good at it. When they asked him what he wanted
for supper he whooped

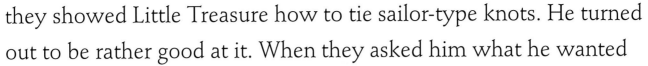

"Swossages!"

and the pirates fell about laughing.
And when it was time for bed, they sang
him off to sleep with a pirate song:

"Captain Abdul's gone to sea,
Silver buckles on his knee.
A pirate life's the life for me,
Bonny Captain Abdul.

"Captain Abdul's brave and bold,
Never does what he is told.
Sails the seven seas for gold,
Bonny Captain Abdul.

"Captain Abdul's fat and fair,
Sails the sea without a care.
He'll come home a millionaire,
Bonny Captain Abdul."

"BOO!"

The next day it was 'Spanish' Omar Lette's turn to baby-sit.

They played hide and seek.

Captain Abdul **"sooperavized"**.

When they asked
Little Treasure what he
wanted for supper he cried
"Swossages!"
and the pirates fell about laughing.
And when it was time for bed
'Spanish' Omar Lette sang him off
to sleep with a pirate song:

"Abdul, he
Had a hook for a hand
And a hook for a hand had he.
He used it to scratch at the fleas in his clothes
And he used it to pick his nose – he did –
He used it to pick his nose…"

"Ow!Ow!Ow!"

cried 'Hard-hearted' Henery Hawkins the following day.
"Take that! Take that! Take that!" squeaked Little Treasure.
Henery had decided to spend his baby-sitting day teaching Little Treasure
the noble art of sword-fighting. BIG mistake! When they asked
Little Treasure what he wanted for supper
he whooped **"Swossages!"**
and the pirates fell about laughing.

And when it was time for bed 'Hard-hearted' Henery Hawkins sang
Little Treasure off to sleep with a pirate song:

"Oh, the Grand old Captain Abdul,
He had ten thousand men.
He sailed them over the seven seas
And he sailed them back again.

"And oh how the ship would rock,
When the jolly-old wind would puff.
And oh how the ship would roll,
When the jolly-old sea was rough.

"And when they were up they were up,
And when they were down they were down.
Ten thousand, sea-sick, going up,
Ten thousand coming down..."

On day four, 'Bully-boy' McCoy and 'Yardarm' Pitts couldn't think what to do with Little Treasure until Captain Abdul suggested they go fishing with him. So, they dangled Little Treasure over the water on a fishhook. **"You dozy pair of kippers!"** bellowed the captain and he sent them to bed without any supper.

When Abdul asked Little Treasure what he wanted for supper he whooped **"Swossages!"** and the pirates fell about laughing.

And when it was time for bed it was the captain who sang him off to sleep with a pirate song:

"Dance t' yer daddy,
My little laddie.
Dance t' yer daddy,
My little lad.

"You shall have a fishy,
On a little dishy.
You shall have a fishy,
When the boat comes in.

"Dance t' yer daddy,
My little laddie.
Dance t' yer daddy,
My little lad."

"Pooh!"

gasped Khan 'the really nasty' on the fifth day.

(Khan was playing 'horsey-horsey' with Little Treasure.)

"He stinks!" howled Khan.

**"Well change 'is nappy, ye great soppy sack
o' seaweed!"** roared the captain.

"No fear!" cried Khan. "I'm not goin' near the rear!"

"It's only poop!" reasoned Abdul.

"Don't blame me!" grinned Percy.

"Give 'im 'ere!" grunted the captain. **"I'll change 'im."**

"No way!" panted Khan. "Not with that hook o' yours –
you'll puncture 'im! I suppose I'll have to do it," and he did!
When they asked Little Treasure what he wanted for supper
he whooped **"Swossages!"** and the pirates fell about
laughing. And when it was time for bed, an exhausted Khan
fell asleep before Little Treasure, so Little Treasure
sang himself to sleep!

This is what he sang:

"Clibbidy clobbidy horsey,
All aroun' d' deck.
Baby dood a poo-poo,
Down d' horsey neck."

Whump!

On day six 'Riff-raff' Rafferty and 'Portobello' Billy taught Little Treasure
everything they knew about gunpowder.

Captain Abdul told them to play something safer, so they played football.

They showed him how to divide up treasure: "One fer you, two fer me…"

They wanted to give him a tattoo, but the captain said he was too young.

"Maybe next year!" he said.

When they asked Little Treasure what he wanted for supper

he whooped **"Swossages!"** and the pirates fell about laughing.

And when it was time for bed they sang Little Treasure off

to sleep with a pirate song:

"This little pirate went to market, this little pirate stayed at home.
This little pirate had roast beef, an' this little pirate had none.
An' this little pirate went 'Ooh-arrgh! Ooh-arrgh! Ooh-arrgh! Ooh-arrgh!'
All the way home."

Kaboom!

The seventh day began with a bang.
"Captain," yelled Percy, as he fell from the crow's nest,
"your wife's back!"

"Oomph!"

gasped 'Bully-boy' McCoy. "I wish you'd stop doing that, Percy."

"Where's me baby?" boomed the captain's wife.

"'Ere! look where yer parkin' that ship!" roared Abdul.

"Watch the paintwork!"

"Where's me baby?" repeated Doris. ***"Where's me little treasure?"***

When Little Treasure saw his mum, he let out a whoop and hooted,

"Mama-ooh-arrgh-avas'-ha-har," and Doris fell about laughing.

"AYE!" cried Captain Abdul proudly. **"I've taught 'im t' speak proper Hinglish. What d' y' think o' that?"**

"Not bad," grinned Doris, ***"considerin' you're as thick as two short gang-planks, ha-har!"***

"Abdul!"

bellowed Doris. *"Come here!"*

She grabbed hold of father and son
and gave them a huge cuddle.

"**GERROFF!**" howled Abdul.

"*Gerroff!*" squeaked Little Treasure
and the pirates fell about laughing.

"*Well,*" said Doris to her baby, "*I can see you've been
well looked after – you look as fit as a butcher's dog!
What've they been feeding you?*"

"Swossages!" whooped Little Treasure
and everyone fell about laughing.

"*Me an' the girls have had a fantastic time,*" said Doris.
"*None of us wanted to come home. Just wait till I tell them
what good baby-sitters you lot are, they won't believe it!*"

Without another word she leaped back onto her ship
with Little Treasure under her arm.

Dumbstruck, the pirates watched as Doris and her crew tied
up their ship and barrelled into town like a horde
of football hooligans.

There was silence on board *The Golden Behind*.

The pirates mooched around the ship kicking things; bored and miserable. The captain told jokes, but no one fell about laughing. Abdul tried to rally his men, but they just weren't interested.

"Truth is, Captain," sighed Percy, "the lads are missing Little Treasure. Aye, he was hard work – much harder than piratin', that's for sure, but everything just seems boring without him."

Captain Abdul had to agree.

That night, a black cloud of gloom hung over *The Golden Behind*.

Kaboom!

"Captain!" yelled Percy as he fell from the crow's nest the following morning. "The ship is full of babies!"

Little Treasure clutched a note. It read: *Dear husbands, as you've done such a good job looking after my Little Treasure we've decided we can trust you*

with all the other kids. We've gone piratin' – ooh-arrgh! Signed Doris and her crew.

"Who would've thunk it?" groaned Abdul, ***The Golden Behind*** **a nursery! I'll be the laughing stock o' the pirate world, ooh-arrgh, that I will, ooh-arrgh!"** But looking at the wonderfully happy sight in front of him he grinned, then roared, **"So what! We're pirates – ooh-arrgh! We don't care what anybody thinks! What d' y' want fer breakfast, shipmates?"**

"Swossages!" whooped the pirates, large and small, and everyone fell about laughing.

That night, when everyone was asleep, full of dreams and
sausages, a certain someone tied a Jolly Roger nappy
to the figurehead of *The Golden Behind*.
"Little tinker!" chuckled Captain Abdul the next morning.
"Big stinker!" hooted Little Treasure.
"Ooh-arrgh, that's my boy!"
roared the captain
and the pirates fell about laughing.

For Nana Dixie, who never got to go pirating

First published 2006 by Walker Books Ltd, 87 Vauxhall Walk, London SE11 5HJ

2 4 6 8 10 9 7 5 3 1

© 2006 Colin McNaughton McNaughton Pirate Schoolbook © 2006 Colin McNaughton
The right of Colin McNaughton to be identified as author/illustrator of this work has been
asserted by him in accordance with the Copyright, Designs and Patents Act 1988

This book has been typeset in Stempel Schneidler and McNaughton Pirate Schoolbook

Printed in China

British Library Cataloguing in Publication Data: a catalogue record
for this book is available from the British Library

ISBN-13: 978-0-7445-7006-9
ISBN-10: 0-7445-7006-9

www.walkerbooks.co.uk

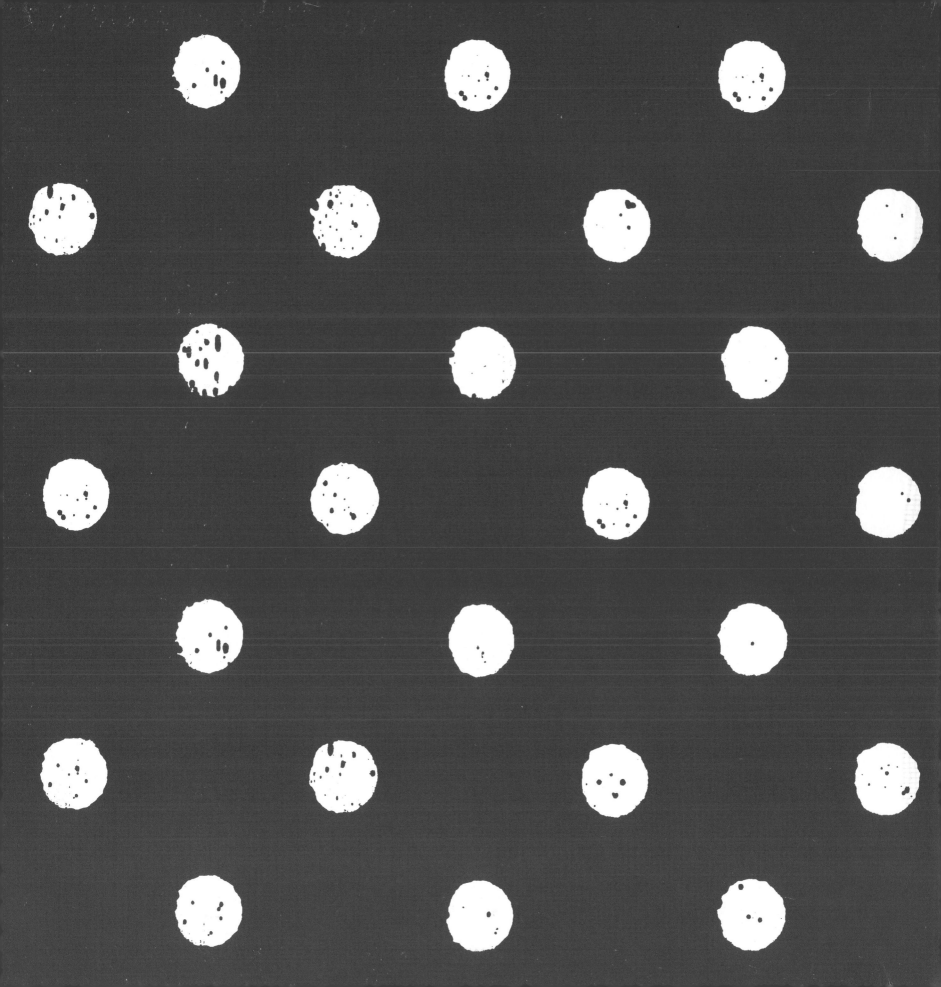